GREAT MOMENTS IN FOOTBALL HISTORY

BY MATT CHRISTOPHER

Little, Brown and Company
Boston   New York   Toronto   London

First Edition

Library of Congress Cataloging-in-Publication Data

Christopher, Matt.
    Great moments in football history / by Matt Christopher. — 1st ed.
        p.   cm.
    Summary: Presents nine of the most famous plays in professional football and the athletes who made them.
    ISBN 0-316-14196-8
    1. Football — United States — History — Juvenile literature.
[1. Football — History.]   I. Title.
GV954.C47   1997
796.332 — DC21   97-1603

10   9   8   7   6   5   4   3   2   1

COM-MO

Published simultaneously in Canada by
Little, Brown & Company (Canada) Limited

Printed in the United States of America

CONTENTS

GREAT
MOMENTS
IN
FOOTBALL
HISTORY

JIM MARSHALL
Only One Game

Have you ever done something so embarrassing you just wanted to disappear? It happens to everybody, even professional football players.

Defensive end Jim Marshall was one of the greatest players of all time. He entered the NFL in 1960 after earning All-American honors at Ohio State.

After playing one season with the Cleveland Browns, he joined the Minnesota Vikings in 1961. For the next nineteen years, through 1979, he anchored the Vikings' defensive line. During his time with the club, the Vikings earned a well-deserved reputation as one of the toughest defensive teams ever.

From the mid-1960s through the early 1970s, Marshall teamed with end Carl Eller and tackles Gary Larsen and Alan Page to form a legendary defensive front nicknamed the "Purple People Eaters" for their bright purple jerseys and their ability to sack quarterbacks.

Over the course of his career, Marshall helped lead the Vikings to four Super Bowl appearances and was an annual selection to the Pro Bowl. If the dictionary needed a picture next to the entry *defensive end,* Jim Marshall would be the top choice.

When Marshall finally retired after the 1979 season, he held a host of NFL records. In his twenty-year career, he played every game of every season, a record 282 consecutive games, including 270 with the same team, the Vikings. Including post-season play, he played in 302 consecutive games.

The closest Marshall ever came to missing a game was when he was hospitalized for nearly two weeks with bronchitis. But he checked out twice — to play football. In 1995, *Sports Illustrated* selected Marshall's consecutive game total as the NFL record least likely to ever be broken.

Another of his NFL records that still stands is his twenty-nine total career fumble recoveries. But Marshall might be happier if that number stood at twenty-eight. One of those recoveries in one of those

282 games was the most embarrassing moment in NFL history.

On October 25, 1964, the Vikings traveled to San Francisco to play the 49ers. Had it not been for Jim Marshall, no one would remember the game today. Neither team made the playoffs that season, and the game had little impact on how either team finished in the standings.

Midway through the first half, the 49ers were pinned down deep in their own territory. At the ten-yard line, San Francisco quarterback George Mira crouched behind the center and barked out the signals.

Jim Marshall crouched on the right side of the line. If the 49ers ran the ball, Marshall was supposed to hold his position. If they passed, he would try to sack Mira.

The ball was snapped. Mira quickly dropped back into the pocket at the three-yard line and looked downfield. He wanted to pass.

The left side of Minnesota's line pushed forward, forcing Mira to step up in the pocket and then move to his right. On the opposite side of the field, Jim

Marshall was sandwiched in a double-team block. He was out of the play.

For a moment, it looked as if Mira would scramble. Then he spotted running back Billy Kilmer open in the middle of the field. Mira threw.

Kilmer (who later injured his legs and switched to quarterback) caught the ball at the twenty-seven and turned to run upfield. He was surrounded by Vikings.

First one player, then another, and finally a third took shots at Kilmer as he spun and twisted at the 30-yard line, trying to get away. As Kilmer struggled to stay on his feet, Jim Marshall headed upfield.

Marshall was unique among defensive linemen at the time. At six-foot-three and nearly 250 pounds, he wasn't just big and strong. He was also fast. Even though he was twenty yards away from the play, he took off upfield in pursuit of the ball. Few other players would have even bothered.

Kilmer's dance gave Marshall time to catch up. As Marshall crossed the 25-yard line, Kilmer, still trying to spin loose, dropped the football.

Marshall's extra effort was about to pay off. As the ball bounced free downfield, he charged in at full speed. He picked the ball up off the ground at the

34-yard line in full stride. Ahead of him, he saw nothing but open space.

It was every defensive lineman's dream. Marshall tucked the ball under his arm and took off.

Only it wasn't a dream. It was a nightmare.

Jim Marshall was running the wrong way!

Somehow, he'd gotten confused. When he'd snagged the ball and seen the open field ahead, he'd forgotten where the line of scrimmage was.

As he reached midfield, the only players chasing him were a few other Vikings, who were hoping to catch up and turn him around. But the 49ers and most of the Minnesota players just stood on the field, dumbfounded. They had never seen a player run the wrong way before.

As he rumbled on, Marshall turned and looked back over his shoulder several times. All he saw were his own teammates, who he assumed were running after him to congratulate him after he scored.

Marshall's long legs ate up the yardage in huge chunks. No one was going to catch him.

When he crossed the goal line into the end zone, he grabbed the ball in his huge right hand and flipped it underhanded toward the crowd in celebration.

Then he turned back to accept the congratulations of his teammates.

They were not smiling.

Then Marshall looked at the referee. Instead of holding his hands parallel over his head, signaling a touchdown, the referee held his arms over his head and placed his palms together, the signal for a safety.

Safety? thought Marshall.

Then it hit him. He realized what he had done. He had run the wrong way and crossed the wrong goal line. When he threw the ball into the crowd, he had effectively downed the football, giving the 49ers two points.

He held his head between his hands and looked for an escape hatch on the field. He wanted to crawl out of sight, fast.

The crowd roared and laughed at the 49ers' good fortune.

But there was nowhere for Marshall to go. After the safety, the Vikings had to kick off to the 49ers. Jim Marshall had to go right on playing.

He felt terrible, but there was nothing he could do about it now. His teammates tried to make him feel better. They knew he was a good player and hadn't made the mistake on purpose.

Marshall took full blame and promised himself to play the rest of the game as best as he could. He wasn't going to let one mistake ruin his career.

In the second half, Marshall went on to play what he later considered to be the greatest half of football of his life. He was everywhere, hounding George Mira behind the line, stuffing the run, and even going downfield again to tackle receivers. Then, late in the game, with the Vikings trailing 22–20, the two-point spread due to Marshall's safety, he got another chance.

The Vikings again had the 49ers pinned deep in their own territory. George Mira faded back to pass. Jim Marshall came charging in. This time, he was moving in the right direction.

Slam! He crashed into Mira, knocking the ball from his hands. It fell to the ground.

Marshall's teammate Carl Eller picked up the ball. With Marshall following close behind and cheering him on his way, Eller rumbled into the end zone for a touchdown. That score was the difference in the game. The Vikings won, 27–22. Now it was Marshall's turn to laugh.

"No one goes through life without making a major mistake," Marshall told a reporter years later. "One of the things I've tried to tell young people is that you can look at a mistake as an obstacle or an opportunity. I took it as an opportunity to prove I was a capable football player. It helped me focus on being the best I could be."

He did that, and more, in the remainder of his record-setting career. After all, it was only one game.

JOE NAMATH
Broadway Joe's Big Boast

Brazen young quarterback Joe Namath of the New York Jets had everyone's attention. Lying alongside the hotel pool in Miami a few days before Super Bowl III, he brashly made predictions as the press gathered around him.

Sprawled in the lounge chair, his long, tousled black hair framing his wide face, he looked as if he didn't have a care in the world.

"We're a better team than Baltimore," he quipped of the Jets' opponents in the game. "[Baltimore quarterback] Earl Morrall would be a third-string quarterback on the Jets," he added.

All around him, the writers scribbled his comments furiously into their notebooks. They knew that once his words reached Baltimore, the Colts would be outraged.

The journalists weren't surprised. Ever since Namath had entered the league four seasons before with a then-record $400,000 contract, he'd been something of a braggart, a player whom some thought was more interested in having a good time than playing football.

But as much as Namath talked, and no matter how much fun he had, he usually backed up his words with his play on the field. He didn't see why the Super Bowl should be different from any other game. He had confidence in himself and his team. He expected to win.

Later that same day, he appeared before the Miami Touchdown Club to accept their award as pro football's most outstanding player. During his acceptance speech, he added fuel to the firestorm his earlier comments had started. "We're going to win on Sunday," he said. Then he paused and added, "I'll guarantee it."

When Namath's comments were reported in newspapers around the country the next day, the experts laughed and snickered. Being confident was one thing, but *guaranteeing* victory? That was an entirely different matter. After all, the Colts were champions of the National Football League. The Jets were only champions of the American Football League. No AFL team had ever beaten a team from the NFL.

The American Football League had been organized only eight years earlier, in 1960. Not until 1967 did the NFL even acknowledge that the AFL existed, when they agreed to meet the AFL champion in the Super Bowl. Thus far, the games had been mismatches. In the first two Super Bowls, the NFL champion Green Bay Packers had easily defeated their counterparts from the AFL.

The two leagues were in the process of discussing a merger, and the Super Bowl was part of that discussion. The NFL wanted to do away with the game, since they felt that the mismatches were detracting from their own championship game.

But the AFL was hoping to change the NFL's mind. Without the Super Bowl, the AFL would lose credibility.

It wasn't looking good for the upstart league.

In 1968, despite the loss of number-one quarterback Johnny Unitas to injury early in the season, the Baltimore Colts supplanted the Packers as NFL champions. Backup Earl Morrall was the highest ranked quarterback in football. He led the Colts to a record of 13–1 and a 34–0 shellacking of the Cleveland Browns in the NFL championship. Some observers considered them one of the greatest teams ever.

The Jets? Well, the Jets had won the AFL with a record of 11–3, then defeated the Oakland Raiders 27–23 to win the AFL championship. But few thought the AFL was as good as the NFL. And Namath, while a talented passer, was better known for his love of the limelight than his ability as a quarterback.

Off the field, Namath was a one-man party. He liked the bright lights of New York, earning him the nickname "Broadway" Joe. He wore his hair long, dressed in colorful clothing, and listened to rock and roll. On the field, he liked to gamble by throwing long bombs to his receivers downfield.

He couldn't have been more different from his counterpart on the Colts. Earl Morrall was a tough, cagey veteran. He wore his hair in a flattop and operated the Colt offense with military precision.

In the days before the game, Namath's comments caused a sensation. The Colts couldn't wait for the game to begin. They thought Namath had shown a lack of respect. They wanted to put him and the Jets in their place.

Even Jet coach Weeb Ewbank was upset when he read what his quarterback had said. "Joe, you know what the Colts are gonna do?" he moaned. "They're gonna put that on the locker room wall. Those Colts are gonna want to kill us."

Namath just laughed. He was that confident. "Coach, you've been telling us we're going to win, right? I just let the rest of the people know what you've been thinking. Don't you think we're going to win?" he teased.

Ewbank could only shake his head and smile. He knew that Namath's confidence was contagious. He had the entire Jet team believing they could win.

Namath remained loose as a goose. When he learned that the Jets would wear their white road uniforms in the game, he quipped, "White uniforms? That must mean we're the good guys."

But few others shared the Jets' confidence. By game time on January 12, 1969, at the Orange Bowl in Miami, the Jets were billed as twenty-point underdogs.

Soon after the game began, it looked as if the point

spread experts had been right. The Jets received the opening kickoff and tried running the ball. They went nowhere. It appeared that Namath was afraid to test the Baltimore defense. The Jets were forced to punt.

Baltimore took over on the twenty-seven. Morrall and the Colts quickly went to work.

Mixing passes and runs brilliantly, the Colts marched down the field. The Jets couldn't stop them, and soon the Colts had the ball on the New York nineteen, first down and ten yards to go.

The jittery Jets suddenly jelled. They harassed Morrall into throwing two incomplete passes, then chased him from the pocket on third down and sacked him for no gain. Baltimore kicker Lou Michaels missed an easy field goal, and the score remained 0–0.

New York took over, but again Namath failed to move the ball. The Colts stalled on another drive, then pinned the Jets on their own four-yard line with a punt.

Now Namath gambled. He threw a risky pass to receiver George Sauer. Sauer caught the ball, but Colt defender Lenny Lyles popped it loose with a vicious tackle. Baltimore took over at the twelve just as the first period was ending.

The Colts' fans roared. From twelve yards out, Baltimore appeared certain to score.

After two plays, it was third and four from the six. Morrall dropped back to pass.

He spotted tight end Tom Mitchell wide open in the end zone. He rifled a pass, but Jet linebacker Al Atkinson barely tipped the ball.

Instead of hitting Mitchell in the chest, where he expected it, the ball deflected behind him and glanced off his shoulder pads. Jet defensive back Randy Beverly made a spectacular interception in the corner of the end zone to give the Jets the ball.

The Colts were stunned. Twice they had had the ball inside the 20-yard line, and twice they had failed to score. A confident Joe Namath led his offense back onto the field.

Four runs by fullback Matt Snell carried the Jets from their twenty to the forty-six. Then Namath took to the air.

He had noticed that the Colts were focusing on wide receiver Don Maynard. Their scouts had obviously told them that he was Namath's favorite receiver. But Namath could do more than just throw deep. Instead of passing to Maynard, he called plays for short passes to his running backs and tight ends.

He completed four of five passes. The Jets moved to the Colts' nine. Then he gave the ball back to Matt Snell.

The big running back scored on his third carry, pushing over from the four. The Jets led, 7–0.

As the Jets celebrated, the crowd was strangely quiet. They couldn't believe that the Colts were losing!

Neither could the Baltimore players. The Jets' touchdown undermined their confidence. The Colts started to press.

Once more they drove into New York territory. From the forty-one, they tried a special play.

Running back Tom Matte took the ball from Morrall and swept to the right. Just as he was about to be tackled, he turned and lateraled the ball back to Morrall.

The play called for Morrall to throw the ball deep to receiver Jimmy Orr. Sure enough, Orr streaked down the far sideline. The Jets were completely fooled. No one was within twenty-five yards of him.

Orr waved for the ball. But Morrall couldn't find him.

He panicked and threw instead toward fullback Jerry Hill in the middle of the field. Jet safety Jim Hudson stepped in front of Hill and intercepted the pass. The Jets had stopped the mighty Colts again!

Now the crowd turned. Instead of cheering the Colts, they started jeering. When Namath took the field to run off the clock before the second half, most of the seventy-nine thousand fans stood and cheered.

The Colts were completely off their game. Instead of trying to win, they were now trying not to lose. Just a few plays after receiving the kickoff to start the second half, they fumbled. The Jets' Jim Turner kicked a field goal. Now New York led 10–0.

Once more, Baltimore failed to move the ball and was forced to punt. New York took over again. Once more, Joe Namath expertly directed them down the field.

He completely out-thought the Colt defense. While they had expected him to gamble and throw long, Namath kept handing the ball to Matt Snell and throwing short passes, eating up the clock and keeping the Colt offense off the field.

Late in the third quarter, the Colts' frustration

peaked. With the ball on the Baltimore twenty-three, Namath dropped back to pass.

For once, his protection broke down. Defensive tackle Fred Miller charged into him and drove him into the ground just as he released the ball, which fell incomplete.

Namath stayed on the ground a few moments. The crowd quieted. When he got up, he trotted off the field, holding his hand.

He'd jammed his thumb. Colt fans hoped that was just the break Baltimore needed to get back into the game.

But Jet backup Babe Parilli stuck to the game plan. Jim Turner eventually kicked another field goal and put the Jets up 13–0.

The Colts turned desperate. They pulled Morrall from the game and brought in Johnny Unitas.

For much of the last decade, Unitas had been the greatest quarterback in football. But after an injury early in the 1968 season, he had sat on the sidelines and watched as Morrall led the Colts to win after win. Now the Colts needed him to be the player they remembered.

It was no use. The Jets were on a roll. They stopped Unitas cold.

When the Jets took over, Joe Namath jogged back onto the field. As soon as the crowd saw him, they gave him a thunderous ovation.

He again drove the Jets down the field. Although the drive stalled at the two, Jim Turner kicked his third field goal to put the Jets up 16–0.

Time was running out for Baltimore. Unitas finally led them down the field for a touchdown, but it was too late. When the Colts recovered an onside kick with just over three minutes remaining, the Jet defense stiffened. New York took over for the final time.

Namath didn't rub it in. There was no sense taking any chances. He stuck to the ground game as the Jets nearly ran out the clock. Baltimore got the ball back for the last time with only eight seconds left. Two plays later, the game ended. The Jets had won, 16–7!

Namath ran from the field with a big smile on his face, waving one finger through the air, signifying that the Jets were number one. The crowd roared their approval. They had come there that day expecting to jeer the quarterback who had guaranteed a win. Instead, they left singing his praises.

In the locker room after the game, a television interviewer cornered Namath and asked, "Did you really expect to win? Or was that just brave talk?"

"Of course I meant it," said Namath. "I always had confidence we would win. I like to have a good time when I play football. When you lose, you don't have a good time.

"So we went out and won."

TOM DEMPSEY
Nothing's Impossible

Impossible.

That's how it looked to New Orleans Saints coach J.D. Roberts and all twenty thousand fans remaining in New Orleans' Tulane Stadium on November 8, 1970. With only two seconds left in the game, the Saints trailed the Detroit Lions, 17–16.

The ball sat on the Saints' own 45-yard line, fifty-five yards away from the end zone. There was time for only one more play in the game.

Roberts considered having quarterback Billy Kilmer throw a desperation "Hail Mary" pass far downfield but decided against it. Plays like that rarely work, and besides, Roberts wasn't even sure if Kilmer could throw the ball that far.

Another option was to try to kick a field goal. But the odds of success were staggering. In 1970, the goalposts were actually on the goal line. With the ball fifty-five yards from the goal, plus the seven yards needed for the snap, the kick would have to travel at least sixty-two yards and clear the goalposts ten feet off the ground.

Roberts thought for a moment. In 1969, Saints kicker Tom Dempsey had kicked a fifty-six-yard field goal, only one yard short of the NFL record fifty-seven-yard kick made by Bert Rechichar in 1957. In practice, Dempsey once made a sixty-five-yard kick. Earlier that day, he had kicked three shorter field goals.

Roberts stopped thinking. "Dempsey," he called out, and looked over to where his kicker stood on the sidelines. "Get in there."

Dempsey looked at Roberts and said quietly, "I'm ready, Coach," then snapped the chin strap on his helmet and jogged onto the field, ready to try to kick a record field goal.

Tom Dempsey wasn't intimidated. He believed in himself. Impossible? Nothing was impossible. In fact, the word had never been in his vocabulary. He had been doing the impossible for most of his life.

Tom Dempsey was born without a right hand and with only half of his right foot, the result of an unexplained birth defect. Apart from that, he was perfectly normal.

He didn't let his birth defects prevent him from doing what he wanted to. His parents gave him lots of encouragement and treated him like any other boy. About the only thing Tom did differently from his friends was stuff wads of tissue into his right shoe so it wouldn't fall off.

He grew up to be big and strong. He was six-foot-one and weighed over 250 pounds. He loved sports. After high school, he attended Palomar Junior College, in California. He wrestled on the wrestling team, threw the shot put on the track team, and played defensive end and kicked on the football team.

Tom was a good athlete, but he knew that it would be almost impossible for him to play defensive end past college with only one hand and half of a foot. He just didn't run fast enough. So Tom concentrated on his kicking. When he was kicking, it didn't matter how fast he ran.

There was only one problem. Tom couldn't find a shoe that would fit his right foot correctly. But that didn't stop him. Instead, he kicked barefoot, and simply covered the stump of his right foot with tape.

After college, Dempsey was determined to give

LAKEWOOD MEMORIAL LIBRARY
LAKEWOOD, NEW YORK 14750

pro football a try. The San Diego Chargers had heard that he was a good kicker and invited him to training camp.

Dempsey impressed the Charger coaches. His kicks were high and long. Many of today's kickers kick the ball soccer-style, approaching the ball at an angle and kicking it with the top of the foot. Dempsey simply stood a few steps directly behind the ball and kicked it straight on.

But the Chargers already had a kicker, Dennis Partee. Although Dempsey didn't make the team, the Chargers were so impressed that they placed him on their taxi, or practice, squad, so he could work on his kicking. They wanted him to try kicking with a shoe, hoping it would improve his accuracy.

The team gave Dempsey a special fiberglass shoe shaped like a normal shoe, but it was too heavy and made his foot hurt. So Dempsey decided to design his own shoe.

He found a shoemaker who agreed to give him some help. After much trial and error, they finally came up with a shoe that fit Dempsey's stump perfectly. With the shoe, Dempsey could practice more. He was kicking better and better each day.

But Dennis Partee was kicking well, too. The

Chargers simply didn't need two kickers. In mid-season, they released Dempsey.

But Dempsey didn't give up. He spent the off-season practicing. In the summer of 1969, he showed up at the New Orleans Saints' training camp and requested a tryout.

The Saints had nothing to lose. Besides, they were curious about Tom Dempsey.

At the tryout, he boomed kick after kick far downfield. Soon other players stopped what they were doing and started watching. The Saints signed Dempsey to a contract. In the exhibition season, he kicked his way onto the football team.

Dempsey had a good rookie year. In one game against Los Angeles, he made a fifty-five-yard field goal, the second longest in professional football history. His kickoffs usually went deep into the end zone. For the season, he made 22 of 41 field goals and kicked 33 extra points, scoring 99 points. With stats like that, people paid little attention to the fact that he had only one hand and half of one foot.

Dempsey and the Saints got off to a slow start in 1970. By the time the Detroit Lions visited them in New Orleans, the team's record was a woeful 1–6–1. Dempsey had made only 5 of 15 field goals. The week before the game, the Saints had fired head coach Tom Fears and replaced him with J.D. Roberts. Dempsey was afraid that if he didn't start kicking better, the Saints might fire him, too.

Dempsey and the Saints played better in the November 8 game against the Lions. In the first quarter, Dempsey kicked a twenty-nine-yard field goal to give the team a 3–0 lead.

But the Lions came roaring back. In the second quarter, they scored a touchdown to go ahead 7–3.

Then the Saints went on a long drive. At the 17-yard line, Dempsey ran onto the field to try another field goal.

But he lost his concentration. He didn't get under the ball, and a Detroit player blocked it, a play that eventually led to another Detroit touchdown, putting the Lions ahead 14–3.

"I just hit it bad and lined it," Dempsey said later. "I didn't concentrate enough."

He soon got a chance to redeem himself. This time, he concentrated and made the twenty-nine-yard kick. Then, just before halftime, he got another opportunity and chipped in a field goal from the eight. The Lions still led, 14–9, but Dempsey had scored all of New Orleans' points.

Neither team scored in the third quarter. In the fourth, the Saints finally made a touchdown. Dempsey's extra-point kick gave the Saints a 16–14 lead.

The Lions came back again. Late in the fourth quarter, they drove almost the length of the field, eating up the clock with runs and short passes. With only fourteen seconds left in the game, Lions kicker Errol Mann booted an eighteen-yard field goal. Now Detroit led 17–14.

Most of the sixty-nine thousand fans in the stands got up and left as soon as Mann's kick split the uprights. Those that did missed a chance to witness history.

Mann's kick took only three seconds off the clock. He kicked off to the Saints with eleven seconds left. New Orleans returned the ball to the 28-yard line. Now just eight seconds remained in the game.

New Orleans quarterback Billy Kilmer threw a quick pass for seventeen yards to receiver Al Dodd. Dodd stepped out of bounds at the 45-yard line with only two seconds left on the clock.

That's when Saints' coach J.D. Roberts turned to his kicker. Dempsey ran onto the field with the rest of the field goal unit to set up the play.

In the huddle, holder Joe Scarpati suggested to

Dempsey and snapper Jackie Burkett that he set up eight yards behind the line of scrimmage instead of the usual seven. Scarpati was afraid that the kick might be blocked. Although moving one yard back would make the kick one yard longer, it would give Dempsey a better chance of getting the kick over the line.

Meanwhile, on the Lions' sidelines, some players were already slapping each other on the back and grinning in anticipation of the win. They weren't worried. After all, no one had ever made a sixty-three-yard kick before.

The Saints broke from the huddle. Scarpati paced off eight yards from the center and knelt on the ground. Dempsey stood next to him and carefully measured off three steps back. He turned and looked to the place where Scarpati would place the ball. Then he signaled that he was ready.

The referee waved his hand. The clock would start running as soon as the ball was snapped.

Dempsey concentrated. He thought of nothing else but kicking the football.

Scarpati barked out the signals. Burkett snapped the ball. The New Orleans linemen charged from their stances and tried to keep Detroit from breaking through.

The snap was perfect. Scarpati caught the ball in front of his right shoulder, deftly spun it around so the laces wouldn't interfere with Dempsey's foot, then quickly set it upright on the ground, holding the end with a single finger.

As soon as the ball was snapped, Dempsey had taken a tiny step with his left foot, then a large step with his right. On his final step, he planted his left foot just behind and to the left of the ball.

Then, with all his strength, he swung his right leg and foot just under the center of the ball.

Boom! It made a sound like no other kick in the history of football.

The Detroit players on the line jumped, hands raised, trying to block the ball.

It tumbled end-over-end just out of their reach.

Dempsey kept his head down, and his right leg followed through and swung up to his shoulders. He took a little hop, then looked toward the end zone.

The ball sailed on a low line, growing smaller, tumbling through the air.

On the sidelines, an official counted down the remaining two seconds and fired his gun. As soon as the ball hit the ground, good or bad, the game was over.

The ball reached its peak, then started down. Players from both teams looked toward the end zone. Scarpati and Dempsey stood together, sixty-three yards from the end zone, watching the ball. *It's straight enough,* each thought, *but is it long enough?*

At the goal line, one official stood behind the goal and another stood even with the goal line so they could tell if the ball made it over. They looked up at the crossbar.

The ball tumbled straight toward it.

All of a sudden, it happened. The ball sailed by, landed in the end zone, and bounced back onto the playing field.

From where Dempsey stood, it was impossible to tell if the kick had been good.

The two officials looked at each other. First one, then the other, raised his hands parallel in the air. The kick was good! The Saints won, 19–17!

Dempsey's sixty-three-yard field goal was the longest in NFL history. The stands erupted with cheers. Dempsey's teammates rushed out to the field and lifted him to their shoulders.

"I knew I could do it," Dempsey said over and over

again with a big smile. "There's so much involved in kicking one that long, but I knew I could do it. All I was thinking about was kicking the ball as hard as I could."

By believing in himself and giving his all to the task, Tom Dempsey had achieved the impossible. But don't tell him that. The word isn't in his vocabulary.

FRANCO HARRIS
The Immaculate Reception

There was less than a minute left to play in the AFC divisional playoff between the Pittsburgh Steelers and the Oakland Raiders on December 23, 1972. Steelers owner Art Rooney slowly rose from his seat in the press box.

As he looked down on the field, he saw the visiting Raiders still celebrating the touchdown they'd scored just moments before to take a 7–6 lead. Even though the Steelers now had the ball, they were pinned back deep in their own territory. Time was running out.

Rooney turned and made his way to the elevator at the back of the press box. He wanted to be in the locker room when the Steelers left the field so he could thank them personally for playing so hard all season long.

As the elevator doors closed, Pittsburgh Steeler quarterback Terry Bradshaw huddled with his teammates on the field far below. It was fourth down and ten yards to go. There was time for just one more play. . . .

Although the Steelers were one of the oldest teams in the National Football League, they were also one of the least successful. They had never won the NFL championship. In fact, they had never even finished in second place or made the playoffs.

But in the early 1970s, the Steelers had begun to improve. Quarterback Terry Bradshaw, in only his third professional season, had developed into one of the best passers in the league. The Steeler defense earned the nickname "the Steel Curtain," because they were so difficult to score on. Rookie running back Franco Harris had rushed for more than one thousand yards in 1972, the first Steeler running back to do so in almost a decade.

Pittsburgh surprised the experts and finished the 1972 season with a record of 11–3. They were champions of the central division of the American Football Conference and qualified for the playoffs for the first time ever.

The Steelers finally had a team their long-suffering fans could cheer for. They called themselves "Franco's Italian Army," after Franco Harris. No one was happier than owner Art Rooney. He had owned the team since 1933, their first season. Now the Steelers had a chance to go to the Super Bowl.

But to get there, the Steelers would have to beat the western division champion Oakland Raiders, one of the most feared teams in football. Defensive back Jack "The Assassin" Tatum keyed Oakland's ferocious defense.

From the opening kickoff, the playoff game had been a defensive struggle. Entering the fourth quarter, the Steelers clung to a slim 3–0 lead.

Midway through the final period, kicker Roy Gerela kicked a second field goal. Now the Steelers led 6–0.

The Raiders were desperate to score. They replaced starting quarterback Darryl Lamonica with young backup Kenny Stabler.

With Stabler at the helm, the Raiders suddenly started to move the football. With less than two minutes left to play, they had the ball on the Steeler 30-yard line. Then Stabler dropped back in the pocket, scrambled, and rolled to his left. All he saw was open field.

He rumbled all thirty yards for a touchdown. Suddenly the Raiders led, 7–6.

Pittsburgh got the ball back after the kickoff and returned it to the 39-yard line. Quarterback Terry Bradshaw tried three passes, but the Oakland defense slammed the door. All three fell incomplete.

That's when owner Art Rooney decided to go down to the locker room. The game appeared to be over.

Down on the field, Terry Bradshaw called one final play, a pass to halfback John "Frenchy" Fuqua.

"I wasn't thinking of a touchdown," Bradshaw recalled later. "All I wanted was a first down." He knew that a field goal would be enough to win. He hoped to get a first down, then move the ball only a few yards more and have Roy Gerela put the ball through the uprights.

It was fourth down. There were only twenty-two seconds left in the game.

Bradshaw barked out the signals and received the snap. He quickly retreated into the pocket as his receivers, including Fuqua, ran downfield.

The Raiders blitzed, and their line put on a tremendous rush. Running back Franco Harris missed a block. All of a sudden two Oakland Raiders were bearing down on Bradshaw.

Just as one reached out for him and started to grab his left arm, Bradshaw ducked and took a few steps to his right. Far down the field, Frenchy Fuqua started to slant in from the left sideline toward the middle of the field. As Franco Harris remembered later, "When the play got messed up, I ran toward Fuqua, hoping he'd get the ball and I could block for him."

Bradshaw stopped and reversed direction. Another Raider was in his path. Now he stepped to his left.

He saw Fuqua open in the middle of the field. As he recalled later, "I cut loose with everything I had on the ball."

The ball shot toward Fuqua at the Raider 34-yard line. As soon as the ball left Bradshaw's hand, he was leveled.

Franco Harris watched the ball pass over his head toward Fuqua.

From deep downfield, Raider safety Jack Tatum watched the play unfold. When he saw Fuqua come open, he started moving in.

Fuqua saw the ball coming toward him like a heat-seeking missile. In full stride, he turned and reached out to catch it.

WHAM! Tatum slammed into Fuqua just as the

ball arrived. Fuqua went sprawling, and the ball ricocheted away.

Franco's Italian Army groaned as they saw the ball sail in the air back toward the line of scrimmage. Then suddenly they turned silent.

At midfield, their hero, Franco Harris, saw the ball wobbling through the air straight toward him. He ran toward it and scooped it off his shoe tops just before it hit the ground.

Ahead, Harris saw only the open field. He tucked the ball under his arm and ran as hard as he could.

Flat on his back, Terry Bradshaw heard a gigantic roar.

Harris was off and running. He picked up one block and took off for the sidelines, glancing over his right shoulder to see if anyone was behind him. No one was. With each step, the din of the crowd at Three Rivers Stadium grew louder.

Only one Oakland defender had a chance to stop him. He tried to cut Harris off at the ten.

He reached out, but his hands slipped off Franco's shoulder pads. Harris sprinted into the end zone.

His teammates rushed to congratulate him. Hundreds of fans poured down onto the field. As Terry Bradshaw remembered later, "When I finally got up, people were grabbing me and I was asking 'What happened?' I didn't know what had happened."

Beneath the stands, Steelers owner Art Rooney was just stepping out of the elevator. He heard a distant roar, and a security guard saw him and yelled out, "You just won!"

Or had he? Down on the field, the game officials were huddled in the end zone. When Harris had crossed the goal line, none of them had signaled a touchdown. They weren't sure if Harris had made a legal catch.

According to the rules in effect at the time, it was illegal for an offensive player to catch a ball after it had been tipped by a player on his own team. The officials had to decide whether Jack Tatum or Frenchy Fuqua had hit the ball. If Fuqua had touched it, the touchdown didn't count.

But no one was sure. Meanwhile, the Steelers were celebrating. Head official Fred Swearingen raced to the press box and met with chief of officials Art McNally. Although there was no instant replay rule at the time, the two men watched a tape of the final play over and over. From the video, they couldn't tell who had touched the ball. And if they couldn't tell . . .

Down on the field, a third official waited by a phone

for McNally to call with his decision. McNally made his decision and barked it into the phone.

The official put the phone down with more than sixty thousand screaming fans looking down at him.

He thrust both arms into the air. Touchdown! The Steelers had won!

Everyone went nuts. The Raiders tried to argue, but it was no use. Tatum later said, "I don't know who touched the ball," while Fuqua allegedly later told some friends on the Raiders that "Tatum never touched it."

It doesn't matter now. The Steelers won and moved on to the next round of the playoffs. Although they lost to the undefeated and eventual Super Bowl champion Miami Dolphins, Steelers owner Art Rooney finally had a championship team. In the next decade, the Steelers went on to win four Super Bowls. Franco Harris's catch became known as "the Immaculate Reception" and is probably the most famous play in pro football history.

WALTER PAYTON
"Sweetness" Sets a Record

They gave him the nickname "Sweetness" because he ran so sweetly.

Chicago Bear running back Walter Payton is the leading rusher in the history of the National Football League. In thirteen seasons with the Bears, from 1975 through 1987, Payton rushed for 16,726 yards, an average of nearly 1,300 yards each season, nearly 3,500 yards more than any other player. Ever.

Payton was everything a running back should be. At five-feet-eleven and just over two hundred pounds, he was strong and tough, with enough power to run over defensive players and get the extra yard when he needed to.

He was fast, too. Over the course of his career, Payton left dozens of linebackers and defensive backs grasping at air after he zoomed past them.

He was also durable. The average career of a running back in the NFL is a little over four years. Most get hurt and are forced to retire. Payton played thirteen seasons and missed only *one* game.

But Walter Payton's best quality was his attitude. He never talked much about his own accomplishments. He preferred to let his running do the talking.

Perhaps that's why the date November 21, 1977, may be unfamiliar. For on that cold, raw November day in Chicago, "Sweetness" did something no other running back in the National Football League had ever done before or has done since.

In one game, across one sixty-minute span of running into and around the visiting Minnesota Vikings, Walter Payton gained 275 yards rushing the football. Twenty years later, his record still stands.

Payton was in his third season with the Bears, whom he joined in 1975 after starring at Jackson State College. In his first season, the Bears used him sparingly. But he broke out in his sophomore season, surprising everyone by running for 1,390 yards. By the beginning of his third year, he was no surprise. But he was almost impossible to stop.

As a team, the Bears posed no such difficulty. Although they had finished the 1976 season at 7–7, their best record in almost twenty years, in the first half of the 1977 season, the Bears were terrible. After losing to Houston 47–0 in late October, their record was a miserable 3–5. They had virtually no chance to make the playoffs.

Yet Payton didn't give up. The next week against Kansas City, his 192 rushing yards keyed a 28–27 win over the Chiefs.

Still, Chicago's playoff hopes were hanging by a thread when the Vikings came to town. The Vikings led the division with a 6–3 record. A win over Chicago would eliminate the Bears from contention and just about clinch the title for the Vikings.

Even worse, in the week before the game, Walter Payton got the flu. On the Thursday before the game, he admitted to being scared that he might be sick with something worse than the flu. He began to feel better the next day, though, and by Sunday, while still weak, he felt good enough to play.

It was cold and blustery at Chicago's Soldiers Field as the game began. For a moment, Payton wondered if he'd made the right decision by choosing to play. But as soon as he started warming up, stretching, and running sprints, he began to feel better.

Payton expected to carry the ball often. The wind was blowing so strong that it made passing dangerous, and Bears quarterback Bob Avellini was having trouble passing anyway.

As soon as the game started, Payton's expectations were confirmed. Each team had trouble throwing the ball. The game soon turned into a battle for field position.

After a scoreless first quarter, the Bears got a break in the second. Pinned back close to their own goal line, the Vikings were forced to punt.

But the wind was too strong. Minnesota's punter got off only a twenty-three-yard kick. The Bears took over at the twenty-three.

Chicago didn't mess around. They handed the ball to Payton. He eventually scored from the one on a sweep to give Chicago a 7–0 lead.

Soon after the kickoff, the Bears got the ball back when Minnesota's quarterback threw an interception. They decided that the safest, most effective strategy would be to keep giving the ball to Payton.

He began to wear down the Minnesota defense. He broke loose for runs of fourteen and twenty-three yards on the drive. He even caught a rare pass for six yards, one of only seven the Bears threw all day, to pick up a key first down.

The drive stalled, however, in Minnesota territory.

But the Bears had the wind at their back. Kicker Bob Thomas took advantage of it and booted a thirty-seven-yard field goal to put the Bears ahead 10–0.

By halftime, Payton had gained more than one hundred yards. Without even asking, he knew he would keep getting the ball in the second half. He didn't mind. He felt strong.

The Bears received the kickoff. By now, the Vikings had figured out that Payton was going to get the ball on almost every play. This time, they stopped him.

On fourth down, the Bears punted into the wind. The Vikings charged hard, and Minnesota linebacker Matt Blair blocked the kick. He then picked it up and ran ten yards for the touchdown. The Bears now led by only three points, 10–7.

With Payton doing the work, the Bears clung to the lead, and the ball. Time after time he went crashing into the line or roaring around the end. Sometimes the Vikings stopped him for only one or two yards, but just as often he broke free for ten or twelve, enabling the Bears to control the football and keeping the Vikings pinned down.

With no more than five minutes left in the game, the Bears had the ball deep in their own territory.

Payton had already carried the ball 37 times for just over 200 yards. One more time, the Bears asked him to carry the ball.

The Vikings were getting tired, but Payton felt fine. Bob Avellini handed him the ball. He broke through the line, then sprinted to the sideline.

He bounced off several tacklers and rolled off another. All of a sudden he was in the clear!

Fifty-eight yards later, the Vikings finally pushed him out of bounds at their own nine-yard line. It was first and goal, Bears!

Chicago still didn't want to take any chances. They tried to run the ball in three times, including one carry by Payton, but the Vikings stiffened. It was fourth down.

In the press box, the newspaper reporters covering the game had started to add up how much yardage Payton had gained that day. He now had 271 yards, only two less than the NFL record held by O.J. Simpson of the Buffalo Bills.

Bears coach Jack Pardee didn't have any idea Payton was so close to the record. Neither did Payton. Both were concentrating on winning the game. Although they were close enough to try to kick a field goal, Pardee called for another run by Payton. He was afraid the Vikings might block a kick and return it for a touchdown. He figured that even if the Bears failed to score, Minnesota would have a difficult time driving into the wind the length of the field to score.

So, for the fortieth time that day, Avellini put the ball in Payton's hands. And for the fortieth time, Payton ran as hard and fast as he could. He swept the end, bounced off a few tacklers, and surged forward to the two-yard line. Although the Bears had failed to make a first down, Walter Payton had just rushed for his 275th yard!

The Bears held on to win, 10–7. After the game, Payton was his usual, humble self.

"What's all the fuss?" he asked the reporters who surrounded him in front of his locker. When they laughed, he said, "You think I'm joking, don't you? I mean it. Records are meant to be broken. It'll happen again. Maybe next year somebody will break it. Fleeting glory."

The only thing Payton did want to talk about were his offensive linemen, the men who had blocked for him. The previous season, when he had broken the thousand-yard barrier for the first time, Payton had bought each lineman a gold watch inscribed with the words, *Thanks for the 1,000 yards, Walter Payton.*

The NFL single game rushing record wasn't the only one Payton set that day. He also set a team record with 40 carries and 1,404 yards for the season.

His spectacular performance got the Bears going. They didn't lose another game in the regular season. Payton finished with a career-best 1,854 yards for the year.

But what Walter Payton did the day *after* he broke the record says more about him than any statistic. With the Bears scheduled to play on Thanksgiving Day, only four days after his record-breaking performance, "Sweetness" didn't take the day off or spend it in the locker room giving interviews. He volunteered to play running back in practice for the scout team, to help the Bears get ready for their next game. He was already looking ahead.

STEVE YOUNG
The Big Run

At halftime on October 30, 1988, the San Francisco 49ers trailed the Minnesota Vikings 7–3. Second-string quarterback Steve Young, playing in place of injured starter and superstar Joe Montana, was the reason the 49ers were behind.

Throughout the first half, the Vikings had chased Young out of the pocket time and time again. Each time they did, instead of following through on the play called by the 49er coaching staff, Young panicked. He scrambled around the backfield, throwing incompletions and being sacked for losses. He finished the first half having completed only four of eleven passes for forty yards. As a team, the 49er offense had gained only seventy-three yards.

In the locker room between halves, the 49er coaches told Steve Young to relax, stay in the pocket a little longer, and rely on the design of the plays.

Each time he scrambled, they told him, he was giving the Vikings a better chance of stopping the 49er offense.

A weary Young nodded in agreement. He was trying too hard, and he knew it. Since joining the 49ers the previous season, the former Brigham Young All-American had patiently waited for a chance to play. At BYU, he had been one of the greatest passers to play collegiate ball. But so far in his professional career, which included two years in the USFL and a year with Tampa Bay, Young had done little to impress anyone. His passing was erratic. He was best known for his mad scrambles running with the football. In fact, some had even suggested that Young stop playing quarterback and become a running back full time.

Young scoffed at the suggestions. He was a quarterback, and a good one. He just needed a chance to prove it. But the 49ers first-string quarterback, Joe Montana, was one of the best quarterbacks in the history of pro football. Young rarely played. In his two years with the team, he started a total of only five games, all when Montana was injured.

The game against the Vikings was Young's big chance. It was an important game for the 49ers. They needed to win in order to stay in contention for a play-off berth.

When Young took the field to start the second half, he told himself to do just what the coaches had said. For a while, it worked.

On the 49ers first possession, he completed five of six passes and took the team seventy-nine yards for a touchdown, putting San Francisco ahead 10–7.

But the Vikings came right back. Only a few plays later, Minnesota quarterback Wade Wilson completed a long pass to receiver Anthony Carter. Carter outran the 49er secondary and scored on the sixty-seven-yard play. The Vikings regained the lead, 14–10.

Minnesota kicked off, and the 49ers took over on their own 27-yard line. On first down, wide receiver John Taylor lined up on the right side. When the ball was snapped, Steve Young dropped back and watched Taylor sprint downfield. Young did just what the coaches wanted him to do. He waited for the play to develop.

Ten yards downfield, Taylor faked inside. At that precise moment, Steven Young faked a throw to the other side. The defensive back covering Taylor went for Young's fake.

That was all the help Young needed. Taylor broke back outside. Young threw a perfect pass that Taylor caught over his shoulder. Taylor raced downfield for a seventy-three-yard touchdown. San Francisco now led, 17–14.

But San Francisco's defense couldn't stop the Vikings, who scored again on a long drive to regain the lead. Entering the fourth quarter, Minnesota led 21–17.

The Viking defense got serious. The first two times the 49ers had the ball in the fourth quarter, they failed to move it.

Fortunately for the 49ers, their defense started playing better. With less than four minutes left in the game, the Vikings were forced to punt.

The 49ers took over on their own 43-yard line with only 3:14 left to play. Everyone on the team knew this would probably be their last chance to score.

Two plays netted San Francisco only eight yards. It was third down and two from their own 49-yard line. The goal line was fifty-one long yards away. San Francisco needed at least two yards to make a first down. If they didn't make it, the game was as good as over.

San Francisco coach Bill Walsh thought the Vikings would expect the 49ers to run for the first down. Instead, he decided to try to fool them with a pass. He inserted an extra wide receiver into the lineup and even had the tight end line up away from the line of scrimmage.

The play called for three of the wide receivers to run pass patterns deep downfield, while the fourth, Mike Wilson, lined up on the left side and cut across the middle for a short pass from Young. Walsh hoped that if Young could get the ball to Wilson, the receiver would have room to run. He might even be able to score.

It was a good play, but it was also risky. Sending four receivers downfield left Young with minimal pass protection. Since the play took a long time to develop, San Francisco's linemen would have to work extra hard to keep the Vikings from sacking the quarterback. And Young would have to be patient.

The 49ers broke from their huddle. As Young crouched behind the center and barked out his signals, he looked out at the Viking defense. Four Minnesota players crouched on the line, while three others stood just a yard or two back, ready to rush. The defense was guessing that the 49ers were going to pass. They didn't plan on giving Young enough time to make an accurate throw.

Young told himself to remain patient. He knew he had to try to stay with the play Walsh had called.

The center snapped the ball, and Young quickly backpedaled as his offensive line formed a protective pocket around him. He paused for a moment, the ball in his hand ready to pass, while he watched his receivers race downfield. On the left side, he saw Mike Wilson cut across the middle.

Sure enough, the Viking secondary followed the three receivers deep downfield. Wilson was coming open over the middle.

Just as Young was preparing to pass, he saw a big purple-and-white blur. Vikings tackle Chris Doleman had slipped a block and was charging toward him, his hands in the air. Young lost sight of Wilson behind Doleman's huge hands.

Young was afraid Doleman would reach up and block the pass. He pulled the ball down and stepped to the side. Doleman tried to stop his charge and tackle Young, but the quarterback slipped out of his hands.

Young looked for Wilson again, but by now the other Viking linemen had pushed past the 49er blockers and were closing in. He spun away and looked for his tight end, Brent Jones, the backup receiver for the play. But he couldn't find Jones in the sea of Minnesota linemen.

Then Young made a quick decision. He had stayed with the play for as long as he could, but there was no one to throw the ball to. If he was sacked, the 49ers would have virtually no chance to win.

There was only one thing he could do. Run!

He first spun away to the left, out of reach of the defensive linemen. Then he cut up field past the line of scrimmage, looking for room to maneuver. But Minnesota safety Joey Browner was closing in.

Head down, Browner took aim at Young and sailed through the air to make the tackle. But at the last second, Young cut toward the sideline. Browner was left grasping at nothing. Young made his way past the first down marker.

He didn't stop. Keith Millard tried to tackle him next, but the quarterback was too fast for the big lineman. Then cornerback Carl Lee took a shot, but Young eluded him, too.

Young kept weaving downfield, twisting and turning, as the entire Minnesota defense tried to knock him off his feet. Each time a Viking approached,

Young somehow cut, spun, ducked, or danced away, still moving downfield.

Young pumped his legs and ran on. Safety Brad Edwards and linebacker Chris Martin each tried to corral him, but Young managed to slip free of both men.

By this time, the 49er quarterback was well past midfield. San Francisco fans were on their feet, roaring with approval. His receivers saw him dashing down the sideline and blocked defenders closing in on him downfield. All of a sudden, Young was in the clear!

But he had run for so long, and had had to stop and start and change direction so many times, that Joey Browner, one of the first Vikings to try to bring him down, had turned around and started chasing him. Young crossed the ten-yard line as Browner closed from behind.

Young's legs felt like lead. Although he had run only about fifty yards straight ahead, he had probably covered another twenty-five while swerving back and forth. He was exhausted, but knew he had to go on.

At the five-yard line, Browner dove through the air and tried to wrap his arms around Young's legs. At the same time Young dove for the goal line, holding the ball in front of him and stretching it toward the goal.

He landed with a thud, Browner wrapped around his ankles.

When Young looked down, he saw that the ball was over the goal line.

Touchdown! The referee's hands shot in the air as the capacity crowd at Candlestick Park roared and cheered. Young's teammates swarmed over him as the Minnesota defenders shook their heads and looked down at their empty hands in disbelief. No one had ever seen a run like that before.

The score put the 49ers ahead, 24–21. The defense shut down the Vikings on their last possession, and San Francisco won.

After the game, Young's amazing run was all anyone could talk about.

The Vikings were heartbroken. "Everyone is going to miss a tackle sometimes," said cornerback Carl Lee, "but you never expect *everyone* to miss a tackle on the same play." Added teammate Issiac Holt, "Young has great athletic ability, but at the same time there was a lot of Keystone Kops on that play."

In the 49ers locker room, there were smiles everywhere.

"Steve looked like a snake zigzagging down the field with lots of people after it trying to kill it," said big San Francisco offensive lineman Steve Wallace with a giggle. "And they couldn't get to it."

Young was exhausted. One of his teammates joked that he "looked like a guy in the desert looking for that last glass of water."

"I've always laughed at people who 'died' at the end of a run," quipped Young, "but that happened to me. My legs died. I'm glad I was on the five-yard line."

The coaches weren't complaining about Young's mad scramble. They knew he had made the smart play. From that moment on, no one questioned Steve Young's ability to play quarterback in the NFL. He had proven he could lead his team. A few years later, the 49ers traded Joe Montana so they could make Steve Young their starting quarterback.

In 1995, as part of the NFL's celebration of its seventy-fifth anniversary, the league selected the greatest run in NFL history. League officials pored over countless hours of film. They watched legends like Jim Brown, Gale Sayers, Walter Payton, and Emmitt Smith all make remarkable runs. But in the end, they selected Steve Young's desperate mad dash as the best.

JOE MONTANA
The Drive

With just over three minutes remaining in Super Bowl XXIII, the Cincinnati Bengals led the San Francisco 49ers 16–13. The 49ers had the ball on their own eight-yard line. The Bengal end zone was ninety-two yards away.

The 49ers stood near their own goal line, waiting for a long television timeout to end. Some players yelled at each other, trying to get fired up. Others were quiet and looked down at the ground, certain the game was already over.

But quarterback Joe Montana was looking toward the fans in the stands behind the end zone. He turned to lineman Harris Barton and said, "Hey, H.," calling Barton by his nickname, "check it out."

Barton was all fired up. He thought Montana had noticed something about the Bengal defense or was going to offer words of inspiration. Instead, Montana simply pointed to the fans in the stands.

Barton gave Montana a puzzled look.

Montana laughed. "There's John Candy," he said. Montana had spotted the comedian in the stands.

"John Candy?" roared a disbelieving Barton. As he recalled later, "There's three minutes to go in the biggest game of the year. And he's so relaxed, he's looking to see who's in the stands."

That's Joe Montana. The player who many believe is the best quarterback ever to play the game may also be the most relaxed player ever to play the game. Perhaps that's why he was able to lead the 49ers to more than thirty fourth-quarter comebacks.

In pressure situations, many players panic. But not Joe Montana. He seems to play even better.

But this was not just any game. It was the Super Bowl. If the 49ers were going to win, Montana would have to be just about perfect.

Earlier in the game, San Francisco had had several chances to take the lead and bury the Bengals, only to make critical mistakes. They missed a field goal because of a bad snap and gave up a touchdown on a kickoff return. Cornerback Ronnie Lott dropped an interception that would have been a certain touchdown, running back Roger Craig had made an untimely fumble, and receiver Mike Wilson had dropped a long pass that would have given the 49ers a first down at the two-yard line.

In most football games, the team that makes the fewest mistakes wins. The Bengals had taken advantage of those 49er errors to take the lead. Victory was in their grasp.

But San Francisco had Joe Montana. That made all the difference.

When the timeout ended, the 49ers huddled. Now Montana was all business. He confidently called out the play sent in by 49er coach Bill Walsh.

Walsh knew that with Joe Montana at quarterback, three minutes was a lot of time. There was no need to try to score a touchdown right away. San Francisco had to move the ball downfield and get out of the hole they were in. Walsh figured that the Bengals would be playing back, trying to prevent the long pass. That would leave the middle open. So Walsh called for a short pass.

Montana took the snap, dropped back, and threw a perfect pass to Roger Craig at the thirteen. Craig put his head down and barreled to the sixteen. Now the clock was under three minutes.

The 49ers stayed with the short pass. On the next play, Montana hit tight end John Frank up the middle for seven yards and a first down.

Walsh noticed that the Bengals were covering star wide receiver Jerry Rice loosely. They didn't want the dangerous receiver to get behind the defense. So he called for a play where Rice crossed from one side of the field to the other underneath the defense.

Joe Montana calmly dropped back and waited for Rice to come open, oblivious to the charging Cincinnati defense. When Rice popped free, Montana hit him with another perfect pass. Rice caught it for another seven-yard gain.

When Rice was tackled, the clock stopped with 1:54 left to play. In just over a minute, Montana had moved the team to the 35-yard line. Now they had some room to maneuver.

Montana dropped back and saw that the Bengals had switched to a man-to-man pass defense. He knew that no one player could cover the talented Rice one-on-one. He threw a pass to Rice down the sidelines. It was good for seventeen yards. Now the 49ers were in Cincinnati territory.

The Bengals were starting to panic. Joe Montana was in a zone. Every pass was perfect.

Now the Bengals decided to go to a zone defense. But Montana found Roger Craig open under the zone in the middle of the field. He threw the ball. Craig caught it for a thirteen-yard gain and a first down at the Cincinnati 35-yard line.

But on the next play the 49ers made a mistake. The Bengals flushed Montana from the pocket, and while he scrambled, one of his linemen drifted downfield. Montana intentionally threw the ball away, but San Francisco was penalized ten yards and lost the down for having an ineligible receiver downfield. It was second and twenty from the forty-five.

Montana went back to Jerry Rice. The Bengals hadn't been able to stop him all day.

Once again, Montana caught the Bengals in man-to-man defense. Rice ran a short slant route over the middle. Montana put the ball right in his hands. Rice caught it in full stride, slipped a tackle, and turned upfield. He gained twenty-seven yards before the Bengals knocked him to the ground. Now San Francisco had a first down at the 18-yard line. Fifty seconds remained in the game.

The capacity crowd at Miami's Joe Robbie Stadium was on its feet. Seven years earlier, Montana had engineered a similar late-game drive to defeat the Dallas Cowboys in the NFC championship game. Was he about to complete another miracle?

The Bengals dug in. They knew that to stop the 49ers, they had to stop Joe Montana.

At the snap, the Bengals line surged forward. It looked as if Montana were in trouble.

Another quarterback might have panicked. Not Montana. As soon as he felt the pressure from the Bengals, he stepped up and the rushing Cincinnati linemen roared past him. Then he saw Roger Craig in the middle of the field. Montana threw.

Craig caught the ball in his midsection, wrapped his hands around it, and was tackled at the ten. Thirty-nine seconds remained in the game.

Coach Walsh sent in a play called "20 halfback, curl X up." Translated into English, that meant that Roger Craig and Jerry Rice were supposed to curl over the middle, while wide receiver John Taylor, on the left side, slanted in farther downfield.

Usually, Rice and Taylor were "double-covered," meaning two players were on each man, and Craig was covered by only one player. Montana often ended up throwing the ball to Craig on the play.

But that didn't always happen. It was up to Joe Montana to look downfield, read the coverage, and throw the ball to whoever was open, usually the player with single coverage.

Montana stood behind the center. Jerry Rice went into motion from the right to the left side. He passed behind Montana and John Taylor, who had split to the left. Montana barked out the signals, took the ball, and dropped back.

Rice sprinted a few steps downfield and curled back. Two Bengals were poised on either side of him.

From the backfield, Roger Craig cut through the line, then turned back toward Montana. One defender waited in front of him. Another moved in from behind.

The Bengals had decided to double-cover both Rice and Craig. The move made sense. Rice had already caught eleven passes for more than two hundred yards and a touchdown, while Craig had caught eight passes for more than one hundred yards. Surely, they thought, Joe Montana would try to throw to either Rice or Craig. The other receiver, John Taylor, hadn't caught a pass all day.

That was just what the 49ers wanted them to think. Cool Joe Montana looked at Craig and saw he was double-covered. As the Bengals rushed in, Montana didn't even bother to look at Jerry Rice. He knew he would be double-covered. That left John Taylor. Taylor was right where the quarterback expected him to be, in the end zone, between the two safeties, a step ahead of the man covering him.

Another quarterback might have faltered in such a tight pass situation. But not Montana. He fired the ball just in front of Taylor, head high.

The receiver reached out and grabbed the ball.

Touchdown! San Francisco won, 20–16. The 49ers were Super Bowl champions once again.

For the day, Montana completed 23 of 36 passes for a Super Bowl record of 357 yards. On the final drive alone he completed eight of nine passes.

After the game, Cincinnati wide receiver Cris Collingsworth summed up the feelings of many when he said, "Joe Montana is not human. I don't want to call him a god, but he's definitely somewhere in between. Every single time he's had the chips down and people are counting him out, he's come back. He's maybe the greatest player who's ever played the game."

And in the 49er locker room, as the team celebrated, Joe Montana simply sat by his locker, smiling, the calmest, most relaxed guy in the room.

FRANK REICH
Un-Bill-ievable Comeback!

The party was starting early.

On the sidelines at Buffalo's Rich Stadium on January 3, 1993, the visiting Houston Oilers watched safety Bubba McDowell intercept a pass thrown by Buffalo Bill backup quarterback Frank Reich. McDowell returned the ball fifty-eight yards for a touchdown, putting the Oilers ahead 35–3 only two minutes into the third quarter.

When McDowell crossed the goal line, the Oilers started slapping hands and congratulating one another. A victory in the first round playoff game was all but certain. All the Oilers had to do was hold on for another twenty-eight minutes. The way the game was going, they thought they just might score another twenty or thirty points.

From the opening kickoff, the Oilers had taken Buffalo apart. Quarterback Warren Moon had shredded the Buffalo defense, throwing four touchdown passes in the first half. Many of the seventy-five thousand fans in attendance left at halftime, certain the game was over.

There were plenty of reasons to believe it was. Buffalo's star quarterback, Jim Kelly, was injured and unable to play. So far, his backup, Frank Reich, making the first playoff start ever in his undistinguished eight-year career, had done nothing. Few fans knew it, but no team in the NFL, ever, had come back from a thirty-two-point deficit to win.

As Houston lined up to kick off after the interception return, Reich turned to his teammates standing around him and said, "We just have to take this one play at a time. That's the only thing we can do."

They glumly nodded in agreement but were hardly inspired.

Yet Frank Reich knew what he was talking about. As a college quarterback for the University of Maryland, his team had once fallen behind to the University of Miami 31–0 at halftime. In the second half, Reich had told himself to take it one play at a time. He had led the Terrapins to a dramatic 42–40 comeback win. All the Bills needed to get going, he thought, was a few breaks.

They got one on the kickoff. Houston kicker Al Del Greco squibbed the ball to prevent the Bills from making a long return. But it hit Buffalo's Mark Maddox at midfield and was recovered, giving the Bills excellent field position.

Frank Reich remained patient. He knew that he couldn't score thirty-two points on one play.

He calmly directed the Bills downfield. The Oiler defense had relaxed a little. They were willing to give up short gains in order to stop the big play. The Bills took advantage of the fact and utilized a series of runs and short passes to put together a ten-play drive. Running back Kenneth Davis plunged over from the one to make the score 35–10.

Yet even though Buffalo had scored, the Bills were in an even deeper hole than before. Running back Thurman Thomas, one of the best players in football, was forced out of the game with a sore hip. He was a major part of the Buffalo offense. His loss made Reich's task that much more difficult.

Buffalo coach Marv Levy decided to gamble. He had kicker Steve Christie try an onside kick.

Once a ball is kicked and travels ten yards, it is a "free" ball. Either team can pick it up. An onside kick happens when a team purposely kicks the ball just over ten yards and tries to recover the ball. If they fail, the other team usually gets the ball in great field position. It's a risky play that rarely works.

Christie squibbed the ball downfield. It took a couple of crazy bounces as he chased after it, trying to beat the oncoming Oiler onslaught. As soon as the ball traveled ten yards, he dove after it and disappeared in a pile of Oilers.

The officials unscrambled the pile, and Christie bounced out, holding the ball. The kick had worked!

Frank Reich went right back to work. On the fourth play, he spotted receiver Don Beebe streaking down the sidelines as the Oilers blitzed. He lofted the ball in Beebe's direction.

The lanky wide receiver caught the ball over his shoulder at the ten and loped into the end zone. Now Houston led by only eighteen points, at 35–17.

The few thousand remaining fans started going crazy. After all, the third quarter was only a few minutes old. There was plenty of time left. At least the Bills had made the game interesting.

The score also energized the Bills. As center Ken Hill told a reporter later, "The momentum shifted our way at that point. You could just feel it."

At the same time, the Oilers started looking over

their shoulders. After Houston received the kickoff, they changed their strategy. They tried to run the ball and eat up the clock instead of playing aggressively. It didn't work. The Bills forced them to punt.

Houston punter Greg Montgomery kicked the ball off the side of his foot, and it traveled only twenty-five yards downfield. Buffalo had the ball in good field position at their own forty-one.

Frank Reich was in his rhythm. He threw an eighteen-yard pass to James Lofton on first down, then hit Kenneth Davis on a screen pass for another nineteen.

Wide out Andre Reed, the Bills' most dangerous receiver, lined up on the left side. When the ball was snapped, he took off down the sideline.

He faked in, then went out. A Houston defensive back moved with the fake. Reed was wide open just inside the ten. He turned and looked for the ball.

Reich rifled a pass into Reed's chest. Reed caught the ball at the five, half-stumbled, then regained his footing and trotted into the end zone. Touchdown, Buffalo! The score was 35–24 with nearly five minutes left to play in the third quarter.

It was the Bills' turn to celebrate. The players on the sidelines turned to the fans and waved their arms in the air. Although only about half the crowd remained, the cheers echoed as if the stadium were full of people. Outside, many of the fans who had left the game turned around and tried to get back inside.

The Oilers took possession after the kickoff and tried to get their rhythm going again. They decided to go back to the passing game that had worked so well in the first half.

But the Bills were on fire. When Oiler quarterback Warren Moon dropped back and threw downfield, Buffalo safety Henry Jones picked off the pass and returned the ball to the Houston twenty-three.

The Oilers defense dug in. They were determined not to let the Bills score again. Their determination paid off.

Three plays netted the Bills only five yards. It was fourth down.

Buffalo coach Marv Levy knew that the Bills could kick a field goal, but he sensed that Reich was on a roll. As he remembered after the game, "I told the other coaches if we hit a fourth [down], we're going for it. I didn't know we'd get a touchdown on the play, but the reasoning was that if we made the field goal, we were still down by eight. The quarter was nearly over and we'd be going into the wind in the fourth quarter, and we'd have to get very close to try a field goal."

So far, the Bills had been throwing to the sidelines. This time, Levy chose a play where Reich threw the ball up the middle.

Reich took the ball from center and quickly skipped into the pocket. Wide receiver Andre Reed dashed downfield and into the end zone, trying to split the two Houston safeties.

Reich threw. With both defenders closing in, Reed reached over his left shoulder and pulled the pass from the sky! Touchdown!

Now the score was 35–31. In less than seven minutes, the Bills had scored an amazing, absolutely unbelievable, four touchdowns, three on touchdown passes by Frank Reich!

Neither team scored on their next possession. Early in the fourth quarter, the Oilers drove deep into Buffalo territory. It appeared as if they had weathered the Bills' comeback and were prepared to resume command of the game.

The drive finally stalled at the fourteen. The Oilers decided to try for a field goal.

Just when the team that had once had a thirty-two-point lead thought nothing else could go wrong, it did. Holder Greg Montgomery dropped the snap. Buffalo took over. The score remained 35–31.

Once more Reich led the Bills down the field one play at a time. Kenneth Davis broke loose on a long run to bring the ball past midfield. Then Reich looked for Andre Reed.

It seemed that Reich couldn't miss. Reed snagged the pass from the 17-yard line and scored easily — putting the Bills in the lead, 38–35!

Now it was Houston's turn to try to come back. Beginning on their own thirty-seven, Warren Moon moved the team downfield as the clock started to run out. With only twelve seconds left in the game, Al Del Greco booted a field goal from the 26-yard line. The score was tied, 38–38. The two teams would have to play overtime. Whoever scored first would win.

Captains of both teams met at midfield for the coin toss to determine who would receive the kick. The Oilers won and elected to receive. The Bills hoped that their string of luck hadn't run out.

The Oilers received the kick and took over at their own 20-yard line. Two plays netted only seven yards.

Then, on third and three, Warren Moon dropped

back to pass. Buffalo nose tackle Jeff Wright pushed past his blocker and took dead aim at Moon.

The quarterback scrambled to get away. Just as Wright reached for him, he launched an awkward short pass downfield.

Buffalo defensive back Nate Odomes didn't even have to move. The ball went right into his hands at the thirty-nine. He took a step, then was tackled by Houston receiver Haywood Jeffries.

The crowd at Rich Stadium went ballistic. As Odomes went down, the referee threw a penalty flag high into the air.

Buffalo fans held their breath. If the call went against the Bills, the interception might be nullified.

The referee stood in the middle of the field and switched on his microphone. As he pulled his right hand down in front of his face, he said, "Face mask, Houston. Fifteen-yard penalty from the spot of the infraction. First down, Buffalo!"

The crowd erupted with cheers as the referee paced off the penalty and placed the ball on the 20-yard line. Frank Reich and the Buffalo offense charged onto the field.

It was no time to take chances. The Bills were already well within field goal range. Reich called for two safe runs up the middle, which netted only a couple of yards. Then coach Marv Levy waved the field goal team onto the field.

Levy was playing it safe. By kicking on third down instead of waiting for fourth down, the Bills could fumble the snap or have the kick blocked, and still have a chance to recover the ball and try again.

Kicker Steve Christie lined up the kick and took a few careful steps back. He signaled that he was ready.

As the holder pulled the ball from the air and placed it upright on the ground, Christie thought only of the place where he wanted to kick the ball. He took three quick steps. *Boom!* His foot found the football.

End over end, the ball spun between the uprights. The referees threw their arms into the air.

The kick was good! The game was over. The Bills won, 41–38!

The Bills players charged onto the field and mobbed each other. The Oilers were stunned. Several Houston players even collapsed to the ground with disappointment.

Frank Reich ran across the field toward the tunnel leading to the Buffalo locker room, his fist pumping through the air. As he reached the tunnel, he was greeted by a sea of hands reaching down from the stands to touch him. He high-fived his way into the locker room, a huge grin on his face.

Not until they reached the locker room did most of the Bills learn that their comeback was not only the greatest in NFL playoff history, but the greatest in the entire history of the league. No team had ever come back from a thirty-two-point deficit to win a game.

The next morning, Frank Reich woke up, turned to his wife, and said, "Did that really happen?" She assured him that it did, and reminded him that he had promised to do a television interview later that morning.

The interviewer asked him if the Oilers had choked.

Frank just smiled. "I wouldn't call it a choke," he responded. "I'd like to give our team credit. We had to shut them down on every count. I don't look at it as a choke. I look at it as a miracle."

A miracle made one play at a time. Un-Bill-ievable!

EMMITT SMITH
Smith Shoulders the Load

On January 2, 1994, the Dallas Cowboys and the New York Giants squared off in Giants Stadium in the sixteenth and final game of the regular season. Although both teams were guaranteed a spot in the playoffs, the winner would be crowned NFC eastern division champions, earn a bye in the first week of the playoffs, and have home field advantage for the postseason. With such stakes on the line, the game was played with bone-crunching intensity.

No one on the field was more intense than Dallas running back Emmitt Smith. Since reaching the NFL after a spectacular career at Florida State, Smith had become the greatest runner in the game and the acknowledged leader of the Cowboys.

On the frozen field that afternoon, Emmitt Smith starred in a performance that still has fans talking. Almost by himself, and despite playing in excruciating pain, he willed the Cowboys to victory.

Late in the second quarter, the Cowboys led the Giants 10–0. With nearly one hundred yards rushing under his belt already, Smith had keyed the Cowboy attack.

He was excited, not only about the chance to beat the Giants but also about his chance to win an NFL record third rushing title in a row. Despite missing the first two games of the season due to a contract dispute with the Cowboys, he had returned to become one of the top rushers in the league. With over thirteen hundred yards apiece, he and Los Angeles Ram running back Jerome Bettis were in a virtual dead heat for the title. A good game now could put Smith in the lead.

Just before halftime, Cowboys quarterback Troy Aikman handed the ball to Smith for the nineteenth time on a play called the "power right." Smith burst through a huge hole carved out by the Cowboys' offensive line and dashed down the right sideline.

Only one man had a chance to catch him. New York safety Greg Jackson had the angle and started closing in. As he did, Smith squeezed the ball tighter and prepared himself for impact.

Crash! Fans throughout Giants Stadium heard the sound of the two men colliding.

Smith tumbled over on his right side, landing heavily on his right elbow. A split second later, Jackson landed on top of him, increasing the pressure on his right side.

A sharp pain shot through Smith's upper arm. He lay on the ground for a few seconds, then slowly got to his feet and trotted over to the sidelines.

At first his arm felt numb, yet after a few moments the feeling slowly returned. Smith wasn't too worried. Most professional football players are accustomed to playing with some pain. He trotted back onto the field and tried to forget about it. Cowboy quarterback Troy Aikman completed a couple of passes, and kicker Eddie Murray booted a field goal as time ran out in the half. The Cowboys hustled off the field with a 13–0 lead.

But when Smith got to the locker room at halftime and started to relax, he realized that the pain wasn't going away. He asked the team trainer to check him out. He had to have help just to remove his shoulder pads and pull his uniform over his head. The slightest movement made the throbbing in his arm and shoulder even worse.

The trainer ordered an X ray, and Smith left the locker room for the trainer's room next door. His teammates watched him leave, concerned.

When Smith returned to the locker room, the other Cowboys were preparing to take the field. He stayed behind, waiting for the report from the trainer. A few moments later, the trainer came out shaking his head.

"You've got a grade-two shoulder separation," he announced.

"What's that mean?" said Smith.

The trainer told him that while the injury was severe, it wasn't as bad as it could be. Smith would be in pain, but there was little chance the injury would cause any permanent damage. If Smith could stand the pain, they could tape and wrap the shoulder.

"Do it," said Smith. If there was no risk of permanent injury, he wanted to keep playing. Although it usually makes no sense to play in any type of pain, particularly for younger players, Smith had played football for years. He knew the difference between playing with pain and just being stupid. It was, as he wrote in his autobiography later, "not about playing hurt. It wasn't even all about helping us win. The main reason I kept playing was to win . . . the rushing title."

Smith's feelings were understandable. Despite leading only 13–0, the Cowboys had dominated the first half, running off 41 plays to New York's 15 and outgaining New York 238 yards to 68. In the second half, Smith expected the Cowboys to take full control and go on to a big win. He hoped to play a few more downs and gain another twenty or thirty yards. Then he'd call it a day, a Cowboy victory and his grasp on the rushing title both secure.

The trainer and his assistant put a pad on his shoulder and wrapped it with tape and bandages. By the time they finished, the other Cowboys were on the field and the second half had begun.

As Smith ran out of the tunnel and onto the field, Giants fans started to boo. They would have preferred not to see the Cowboys' star running back return to the lineup. But soon their jeers would turn to cheers.

At midfield, the Giants were forced to punt. Cowboy safety Brock Marion partially blocked the kick, which spun crazily only eighteen yards downfield. Cowboy return man Kevin Williams fielded the ball but fumbled. The Giants recovered on the thirty-nine. New York was on the move.

They quickly banged in for a touchdown, making

the score 13–7. All of a sudden, the Cowboys were in a tighter ball game.

Smith's priorities changed. From that moment on, he said later, "I never even considered the rushing title. I was out there to win."

Since Smith had done so well in the first half, the Cowboys decided to keep using him. They got the ball back, and they put it in his hands the first play.

Clutching the ball tightly, Smith swept to the right side, turned the corner, and ran out of bounds for a nine-yard gain. Luckily for his throbbing shoulder, he didn't get hit on the play.

But Smith knew his luck wouldn't last forever. The Giants were too good, and they knew he was hurt. Their best chance to win would be to knock him out of the ball game.

The Cowboys handed the ball to Smith again. This time he ran left. But he was cut off from the sideline. He turned back inside and looked for room to run.

What he found were a couple of New York line-backers.

Crunch! They smashed into his sore shoulder and sent him reeling. All of a sudden, Smith's shoulder felt as if it had just been injured all over again.

He returned to the huddle in obvious pain, his right

arm held close to his body. His teammates wondered if he would be able to continue.

He did, but his deteriorating condition fired up the Giant defense. They forced the Cowboys to punt. Then the Giants kicked a field goal to make the score 13–10.

Dallas tried to adjust. Instead of running Smith inside, they sent him wide on sweeps so he wouldn't get hit straight on.

Although the strategy protected Smith, the Cowboys' offense stalled. The two teams settled into a defensive battle.

For the remainder of the third quarter and for the first half of the fourth, neither team moved the ball effectively. Then the Giants took over deep in their own territory.

Running back Rodney Hampton carried the ball for nine of twelve plays, and the Giants pushed down the field. With only seconds left, and the ball on the Cowboy fourteen, New York kicked a field goal to tie the game at 13–13.

Moments later, the clock ran out. After a brief rest, the two clubs would have to play overtime.

Oh, no, thought Smith, *that's just what I need.* He had barely made it through the fourth quarter. While trying to protect his shoulder, he had allowed himself to be hit in the chest and side. Now, in addition to the shoulder injury, he had bruised his breastbone and ribs. He should have been on his way to a hospital. Instead, he knew he had to keep playing. The team needed him.

He tried to ignore the pain that wracked his body. He knew that if he left the game, the Giants would receive a huge emotional lift. He had to keep playing, he later remembered, "if only to pose the threat of a running game." He hoped that his presence on the field would force the Giants to guard against the run, allowing quarterback Troy Aikman to throw the ball downfield.

But first the Cowboys had to get the ball. The Giants won the toss and chose to receive. As soon as they did, they started driving. A penalty for an illegal block finally stalled them, and New York was forced to punt. The Cowboys took over at their own twenty-five.

In the huddle, all eyes were on Smith. His teeth were clenched, and he moved stiffly.

"Emmitt, you okay?" asked one of the Cowboys.

"I'm fine!" yelled Emmitt. "Leave me alone!" He

didn't want to be reminded of the pain, which was now so bad he had bitten through his mouthpiece. He just wanted to win.

That's what the Cowboys wanted, too. As they had so many times in the past, they turned to their all-Emmitt offense.

Time after time they put the ball in his hands. Running inside as well as outside, Smith shredded the Giants' defense, then pushed forward for more yardage with two or three defenders draped over his back.

Even when the Cowboys decided to pass, they still put the ball in Smith's hands. He caught three passes on the drive for twenty-four yards.

As he broke through the line of scrimmage on one play, star linebacker Lawrence Taylor, one of the hardest hitters in the league, moved in to make the tackle.

Without thinking, Smith raised his sore right arm, placed it under Taylor's chin, and stiff-armed him away. Pain shot through his body, but Taylor fell away and Smith picked up several more key yards. "I wasn't thinking," Emmitt said after the game. "It was just a reaction."

After another play, Smith turned to Cowboy guard

Nate Newton and said to the big lineman, "Run behind me and pick me up. I don't want to lie on the ground." Newton nodded in admiration.

Just past midfield, Smith got crunched between two Giants and finally staggered from the field. The crowd applauded in grim appreciation of his monumental performance.

But they hadn't seen the last of Smith. One play later, he returned and ran for ten more grueling yards. He looked to the sidelines and saw that the Cowboys were within field goal range. He had done what he'd set out to do. "Get me out of here!" he called to the Dallas bench.

The field goal unit charged onto the field as Smith stiffly walked off. Placekicker Eddie Murray drilled a forty-one-yard field goal, and the Cowboys won, 16–13. Emmitt Smith's day was done.

For the game, he had gained an amazing 168 yards on 32 carries, plus another 61 on 10 pass receptions. Of Dallas's 70 offensive plays, Smith had handled the ball on 42, gaining 229 of the team's 339 yards. On the final game-winning drive, he had handled the ball on nine of the team's eleven plays and gained 41 of their 52 yards.

"I don't know how he did it," admitted Cowboy

guard Kevin Gogan after the game. "He sucked it up for his boys."

After the game, an obviously pained Emmitt Smith met with reporters and explained his decision to keep playing. All he was thinking of, he said, was winning the game. Then he finally allowed himself the luxury of thinking of the second thing he'd achieved that day — winning his third rushing title. "Those are two things I can someday look back on and say, 'Emmitt, you did a heck of a job.'"

When a reporter asked Smith if he would be able to play in the first game of the playoff just two weeks away, he managed a smile. "There's no way they'll keep me out of it."

Of that, no one had any doubt.

Read them all!

All available in paperback from Little, Brown and Company

Matt Christopher

12.96

	DATE DUE		
JUL 2 3 200			